SAMMY'S SPOOKTACULAR HALLOWEEN

MIKE PETRIK

two lions

Extra special thanks to Mom and Dad,
Teresa Kietlinski, Kelsey Skea, Merideth Mulroney,
Candace Fleming, Eric Rohmann, Matthew Cordell,
Stacy Curtis, Chris Sheban, Larry Day, Tom Lichtenheld,
Mark Winter, Chris Roman, John Courchane, Adam Marzec Sr.,
Joe Grock, and Ethan Barnowsky

Published by Two Lions, New York
www.apub.com
Amazon, the Amazon logo, and Two Lions are trademarks of Amazon.com, Inc., or its affiliates.

ISBN-13: 9781503901797
ISBN-10: 1503901793

The illustrations are rendered in digital media.
Book design by Tanya Ross-Hughes
Printed in China
First Edition
10 9 8 7 6 5 4 3 2 1

For Ali

Halloween was a ghoulishly delightful
time of year for the Loomis family.

They had the biggest, creepiest, jump-scariest
haunted house in the neighborhood.

Haunted House

The whole family took part in the spooky celebration.
Dad was the Halloween Spirit, and
Mom and Molly were cackling witches.
Luke made the lightning flash,

the thunder crash,

and the fog roll.

And Sammy made sure to give
the trick-or-treaters
a fang-tastically fun time.

You see, Sammy **LOVED** Halloween.
The candy. The pumpkins.
The scares.

He wished Halloween lasted all year long.

Every year, on the morning after Halloween, the Loomis family celebrated with a mountain of pumpkin pancakes.

But this year, Sammy was too busy to wolf down pancakes. He was already cooking up ideas for next year's haunted house.

"You're too little to come up with anything creepy or cool!" teased Luke.

"Even if you have a whole year," said Molly.

"Hold on now, kids," Sammy's dad said.
"We can always use some shocking new scares.
Sammy, why don't you give it a whirl?"

"YES!"

cried Sammy.

"I won't let you down!"

Sammy got right to work.
After a few weeks of planning,
he started testing some ideas.

"Hello? Anyone down here? I can't see a thing!" said Mom.
"Hmm," said Sammy. "Maybe a tad too much fog fluid . . ."

Not everyone liked
his freakishly fun improvements
to Thanksgiving . . .

Gobble

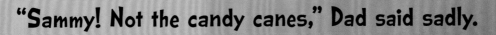

"Sammy! Not the candy canes," Dad said sadly.

"Dude, that's my stocking," cried Luke.

Over the winter, Sammy's creations grew more
and more scare-ifying.

Every birthday party,
sleepover, and
family celebration
saw the testing
of new ideas.

SODA

ODA

DA

By Easter, Sammy was on a roll.
He was thrilled with
his haunted house progress.

"MOMMY!"

But when Sammy cooked up
a monster storm at the
Fourth of July barbecue,
his family had had enough.

"FIRE BAD!"

"Your ideas are wonderfully creepy," said Dad,
"but Halloween has taken over everything.
Until the rest of the family is ready, no more haunting!
No more spooking! And no more Halloween pranks!"

Sammy realized he had gone too far.
"I've ruined everything," he said.
"I give up. No more Halloween."

"Well, not everything was ruined," said Luke.
"That slumber-party skeleton will leave those
trick-or-treaters shakin' in their boots."

"And those tarantulas were a gruesome
good time," Molly added.
"Did you see how fast Luke ran from them?"

"Looks as if you could use some help," Luke continued.
"C'mon, let's get to work."

And they did.

As the last spiderweb was hung, Mom and Dad were spellbound.

"They were Sammy's ideas," said Molly.

"Yeah, we just helped," said Luke.

"Sammy," said Dad, "even though you zombie-chomped the Christmas presents and rattled bones at all our parties, we admire how you've stuck with it all year long."

"Especially how you worked with Molly and Luke to make it all come together," added Mom. "So we're naming you Halloween Spirit this year."

When Halloween night arrived, Sammy was ready.

"HAPPY HALLOWEEN!

he cried.

"And welcome
to the Haunting
at Oakwood Farms.

Come in, but beware of
what lurks in the dark.
Muah ha ha!"

Every hair-raising scare was
more terrifying than the last.

When the last of the trick-or-treaters had shuffled off,
the family had one last Halloween trick.

And this time
it was for **Sammy**.

"GOTCHA!" his family cried.

"That was one good jump scare, everyone,
and this was the best Halloween ever.

But maybe next year we could use the whole house!
Molly, we can start in your room. Who's in?"